The Tale of

HIGHOVER HILL

Other titles by Penny Dolan:

The Tale of Rickety Hall

The Tale of

HIGHOVER HILL

Penny Dolan
Illustrated by Wilbert van der Steen

A Jonas Jones just for Jim!
With love and many thanks for all
your help along the journey.
Penny

Scholastic Children's Books,
Commonwealth House, 1-19 New Oxford Street,
London WC1A 1NU, UK
a division of Scholastic Ltd
London ~ New York ~ Toronto ~ Sydney ~ Auckland
Mexico City ~ New Delhi ~ Hong Kong

Published in the UK by Scholastic Ltd, 2002

Text copyright © Penny Dolan, 2002
Cover illustration copyright © Klaas Verplancke, 2002
Illustrations copyright © Wilbert van der Steen, 2002

ISBN 0 439 98235 9

Printed and bound in Great Britain by
Cox & Wyman Ltd, Reading, Berkshire
Typeset in Horley Old Style

2 4 6 8 10 9 7 5 3 1

chapter 1

Years ago, an ancient house stood high on a hill, half hidden by trees. The house was known as Rickety Hall. Its tall tower and chimneys seemed to tell of secrets and stories, even on a bright winter's day. . .

* * *

The morning sun glinted across the snow-covered land. At the foot of the wide stone steps of Rickety Hall sat an old-fashioned sledge. It was made of wood and iron. Three huge hounds – Ruff, Tuff and Greytail – stood in the leather traces, breathing small clouds into the frozen air. Ruff and Tuff rattled restlessly at their harness but Mother Greytail soon growled them to order.

The massive door of the ancient house creaked open. Out ran a lad with a long scarf wrapped around his neck and a long list in his hand. The boy was Jonas Jones. At his heels pattered a small stubby-tailed mongrel.

"Come on, Scraps," said Jonas, shoving the list into his coat pocket. "We've a right load of things to bring back today."

Jonas climbed swiftly into the driving seat, and Scraps jumped in beside him.

Jonas glanced up at Rickety Hall. Five old men, each older than the one before, had popped up at the windows. They waved urgently, wishing Jonas a safe return. Beside each was a friendly dog, pressing its wet nose against the glass. Scraps wagged a stubby tail at his furry friends, and Jonas waved confidently back at his rather unusual family. Then he twitched the reins lightly, and the hounds began to pull.

The sledge moved slowly across the snow, sliding between several strange-shaped bushes. Then it gathered speed, and the hounds were soon racing away down the drive. The tight right turn at the stone gateposts swooshed up a flurry of snow, but that was part of the fun.

On they went, passing snowy fields and frosted hedges. Scraps sat beside Jonas, sniffing the breeze. Jonas felt the air cut chill against his face and fingers, and he shivered. Once with the cold, and once remembering the time before Rickety Hall had been his home.

Jonas thought of the freezing days and bitter nights when he and Scraps had been homeless, starving in the winter's frost. Jonas shuddered, recalling the gloating cries of the evil Dog Catcher, and the terrible net tugging tightly around them. Ah well, at least that time was over. Deep within the folds of his warm scarf, Jonas smiled thankfully. He reached one hand over and ruffled Scraps's furry back.

"Woof!" the little dog replied, wagging his stubby tail.

* * *

The little town of Riddlesden lay just below Rickety Hall, but Jonas and Scraps weren't going there today. Today's trip was across the moor to the very top of Highover Hill. From there, a long steep bank led the road into the town of Hebbing Bridge, with its barges and waterways.

Jonas grinned at the thought of that long, swift slope. He'd be driving the sledge down it himself – for the very first time! He could hardly wait. He knew that the journey back up the hill wouldn't be so easy. Then the sledge would be loaded with parcels, and he'd have to walk beside the hounds.

Jonas held the long reins tight, as the hounds' strong paws pounded through the crisply frozen snow. Bit by bit, the moorland road rose a little more steeply, until the land dropped away and they reached the crest of Highover Hill.

Ruff, Tuff and Greytail knew the road, and drew to a halt. They waited, with tails wagging wildly, while Jonas walked all around the sledge. He checked the hounds were safe in their harness. He checked that the wooden brakes were good.

Far below them lay the stone-roofed houses of Hebbing Bridge, with the river looping between the buildings like a ribbon of ice. Rows of boats and barges were tied along its banks, caught by the sudden grip of winter.

Jonas eyed the slippery slope of Highover Hill carefully, and was just climbing back on to the sledge when something caught his eye.

Perched right on top of the old milestone was a girl with a mane of fiery red hair. Even though the air was cold as ice, she stood there, balancing on one leg like a statue.

Her arms were stretched out like wings, as if she was longing to leap into the sky.

Jonas couldn't help noticing her angry face, her pale cheeks and thin, starved wrists. He remembered those days when he had looked much the same.

"Hello…" he began.

Immediately, the girl turned, jumped down and spat at him.

chapter 2

"What are you staring at?" she scowled. Jonas kept on staring. The girl looked about his own age. A thin, embroidered shawl covered her ragged clothes.

"Staring at you," he told her straight enough. He wasn't having anyone talk to him like that. "Nothing wrong with that is there?"

"There is," she said, bitterly, "when you get gawped at half the day already!" The girl turned away, hunching her shoulders as if all thoughts of flight had been folded away.

Jonas paused. "You all right?" he asked, more gently.

"What's it to you, eh? What's it to anyone?" she muttered, and tossed her head.

"Don't know unless you tell me, and that's the truth of it," Jonas answered calmly. "Anyway, I was going to ask you if you wanted a ride down to Hebbing Bridge? Do you? My name's Jonas Jones."

He seized the reins, and the hounds rose to their full height. The girl gazed at their thick grizzled coats and strong determined heads, as if she trusted them to carry her safely. But she still eyed Jonas with suspicion.

"Woof, woof!" said Scraps, bouncing down from the sledge and scampering towards her. His tail wagged in such a friendly way that the girl couldn't help smiling.

"This is as far as I can go," she sighed, "so yes, Jonas Jones, I'll join you!"

She jumped in beside Jonas. Scraps squashed his warm body between them, and licked the girl's cold hand. She patted his little head in return.

The girl's face grew serious. "Don't take me right into town, Jonas. Promise? I mustn't be seen."

Jonas wondered about this strange girl. Maybe she was a runaway servant? Or worried by the workhouse? He certainly didn't think anyone was looking after her – not properly, for sure. He'd noticed the bruises around her ankles.

"Nobody will see you," Jonas told her. "I'll have to slow the sledge long before the knobbly cobbles of Hebbing Bridge anyway."

Jonas gave a sharp whistle, and Ruff, Tuff

and Greytail were off. The sledge shot down the long hill, swift as a weaver's shuttle. Jonas steered it steadily between the curving banks, and it felt like heaven.

Jonas glanced across at his passenger. Her bright eyes smiled back, dancing with excitement as the sledge sped faster and faster. They began laughing with the thrill of the ride. All at once, the girl threw back her head and started singing. Her voice was clear and strong.

Down, down, they went – the trees and hedges flashing past them – down, down, until they reached the foot of Highover Hill and met the low road. Jonas brought the dog-sledge to a halt just by Hebbing Common.

"Best thing for ages, and that's the truth," the girl said, smiling broadly as she skipped off the sledge. "Thank you, Jonas Jones." Then she tipped her head to one side, and held out a thin hand. "Hey, you got anything to eat?"

Jonas grinned, reached into his pocket and brought out a couple of rosy apples. She grabbed them urgently, thanked him, and was off, racing across the Common.

Jonas watched her go. She headed for the distant side where, almost in the wood, someone was camping. Jonas spotted a once-handsome caravan, but now the paint was peeling off the wooden frame. Close beside it stood a small cart, roofed with canvas. Someone had strung old blankets beneath the caravan, making a rough shelter from the weather. Strange smells came wafting across on the wintry air, and Jonas heard a clinking and a clattering, and harsh voices chattering.

Nearby, a small donkey and an old horse grazed hungrily on the winter-hard grass. They lifted their tethered heads as the girl ran towards them. She stroked their necks fondly, and held out the apples for them to munch.

At once there was an impatient volley of shouts.

"Lizzie Linnet! You'll come here now if you know what's good for you."

The girl seemed to shrink into herself as she walked sullenly towards the caravan, and disappeared. There came a quick cry, followed by an angry voice. Jonas listened.

"Been wasting time dancing and prancing girl, when there's work to be done before noon?" someone shouted. "You weren't thinking of running off, were you, girl? Because you can't!"

"I know, I know," came Lizzie's plaintive reply.

"Then get on with your tasks! Breakfast's already eaten," the harsh voice ended.

Jonas frowned, and found himself worrying about poor Lizzie. He had a very bad feeling about whoever had made that raggedy camp. They certainly weren't the travellers who usually camped at the Common.

"Woof?" asked the little dog, nuzzling beside him.

"Don't know, Scraps," Jonas said, taking up the reins of the sledge again, "but it don't look good."

chapter 3

Jonas steered the sledge into Hebbing Bridge, towards the busy river. Ruff, Tuff and Greytail edged slowly through the snow-rutted streets.

Boats and barges were moored all along the banks, imprisoned by the icy waters. All the same, goods had to be unloaded, so carts full of crates and barrows stacked with bundles were wheeling off in all directions.

Jonas led the sledge into the yard of their usual warehouse. He tethered the hounds. Then he hurried into the building, and into the office.

The man behind the desk gave a chuckle. "Hello, young Jonas. Come for your packages, then?" Taking the pencil from behind his ear, he checked the scribbled pages on the order-book. "Yes. Everything's arrived, and just in time, too. There'll be nothing moving on the water for a while in this weather."

It took some time to collect every item up. There were parcels of pen-nibs, paints and piano-strings, boxes of books, boots and bed-shirts, and masses of maps, manuscripts, music and all manner of things, all for taking back to Rickety Hall.

The man gave Jonas a hand, but still it took a while to load the back of the sledge, and to fasten the covers down safely too. When everything was secure, Jonas brought the hungry hounds a late breakfast of bones and biscuits.

Then he eyed the sky. The sun was shining like a brass button high in the cold blue sky, and the day was bright. But Jonas knew that once the sun started to set on winter afternoons, the moors grew dark and cold quickly.

"Reckon we can wander round town for an hour or so, Scraps," he decided, "but we must set off in good time to get back to Rickety Hall."

Jonas set the hounds to guard the sledge, and then the boy and his dog set off to find something tasty for themselves too.

They left the river and the warehouses, and made their way up Main Street, which was thronging with people. Jonas bought two golden-crusted pies from the back window of the Weavers Arms, one for himself and one to share with Scraps.

Then he searched for a corner so they could munch their lunch comfortably. As they ate, Jonas noticed that several folk were nosing at a yellow poster pinned outside the Weavers Arms. Wiping the crumbs from his mouth, Jonas went over to have a look too. He stared at the poster and read:

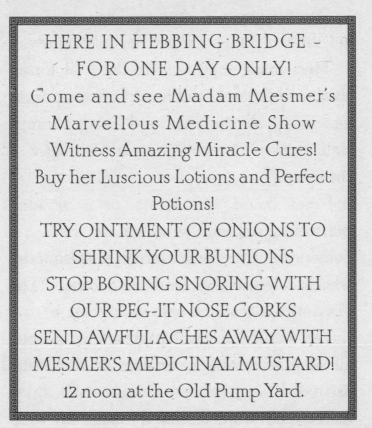

HERE IN HEBBING BRIDGE –
FOR ONE DAY ONLY!
Come and see Madam Mesmer's
Marvellous Medicine Show
Witness Amazing Miracle Cures!
Buy her Luscious Lotions and Perfect
Potions!
TRY OINTMENT OF ONIONS TO
SHRINK YOUR BUNIONS
STOP BORING SNORING WITH
OUR PEG-IT NOSE CORKS
SEND AWFUL ACHES AWAY WITH
MESMER'S MEDICINAL MUSTARD!
12 noon at the Old Pump Yard.

Jonas looked at the clock on the church tower. It was almost midday now. He rattled the coins in his pocket. Rickety Hall was a rather chilly place in winter, and the cold draughts brought plenty of aches and pains to his old men.

"Worth a look, eh, Scraps?" he said.

"Woof!" Scraps wagged his tail brightly.

They made their way to the Old Pump Yard, and Jonas scrambled up a fence-post to peer over all the hats and heads. Scraps settled down to snooze against the shelter of the fence.

Jonas could see across to a wooden platform, draped with gaudy banners. Something rather like a small wardrobe on wheels stood in the centre of this stage. The doors were decorated with strange signs.

The Pump Yard was packed with people, all chattering and pointing at the stage excitedly. They hushed when a small, thin-haired man climbed on to the stage. He wore a pair of buckled boots, and an enormous coat dragged behind him, large enough to fit someone twice his size. It was plentiful with pockets.

A smile stretched across his mean-eyed face as he bowed low. "Octodious Ollett, Ointment Blender, at your service!"

He edged along the stage, reached into a greasy satchel, and flung copies of the yellow poster to the crowd. Suddenly some blue posters fluttered out from the satchel too. Ollett grabbed at them anxiously, and caught all but one.

The wind whirled the blue poster towards the fence where Jonas perched. It twirled around and down and landed lightly on Scraps's nose. Startled, the little dog seized it neatly between his teeth. Ollett leapt down from the stage, and pushed his way through the crowd. He was after his blue poster. He bent down to Scraps.

"Give that back to me, you sweet little doggie!" he wheedled.

Scraps did not like this man and he did not feel like being sweet. If Jonas hadn't been so close, Scraps might not have been so brave, because the little man's boots were surprisingly large. Scraps held on to his blue poster and backed away, growling. He wouldn't give it up.

But the church clock was striking noon, and the waiting crowd began to stamp and shout. Ollett tried one last snatch, but Scraps was too quick for him. Mumbling curses, Ollett clambered back on to the stage. Quickly Jonas calmed Scraps, stuffed the poster into his pocket for later, and climbed back up the fence again. The show was starting!

Ollett flung off his coat to reveal a suit of velvet patches and rusting tinsel. He took out an ill-tuned pipe and started to play.

A nimble figure danced on to the stage, sparkling in sequins and spangles. Her face was half-hidden by a black velvet mask. The figure flipped upside down, and ran along on her hands. She twirled and whirled in cartwheels. She turned triple somersaults, higher and higher and higher, faster and faster.

The crowd gasped with amazement at her brilliance. At last, as she paused, balancing on one leg, with arms outstretched, Jonas recognized her. It was Lizzie Linnet!

Ollett, clumsy as a toad, blew a croaking finale on his pipe. Then he began to speak.

"Ladies and Gentlemen, you have just seen the Famous Dancing Princess of Perapsia! Once the Princess was a poor, bedridden thing. But thanks to the wonders of Mesmer's Medicinal Compounds, she dances as you saw before you this very hour!"

The Dancing Princess curtseyed, and left the stage, with the crowd clapping her loudly.

"Now," continued Ollett, "I present the Star from Afar, the Quack with the Knack, the Marvellous Madam Mesmer!"

chapter 4

On to the stage slunk a tall woman. Shimmering robes swirled about her thin body. A row of amethysts clung around her throat. She was crowned with a silken turban, and held a long ebony cane.

Her face was pale as ice, and her eyes were a deep, dark liquid purple. They were, Jonas thought, the largest eyes he'd ever seen. There was something quite horrible about them. Madam Mesmer pointed her long ebony cane at the crowd, and they grew silent. Then she handed the cane to Ollett.

She reached into her robe, and extracted an enormous glass crystal. It hung from a golden chain. As she snaked across the platform, the brilliant stone flashed to and fro, to and fro in time to her movements.

"Trust in me!" Madam Mesmer's entrancing voice began. "Oh, have no fear! Soon those terrible pains will disappear!" she sang, winding her way across the stage. "Yes, trust in me! Every spoon or drop" – she smiled enchantingly – "will bring your aches to a stop! Oh, trust in me! You will not feel worse," she breathed. "Just give a coin or two from your brimming purse!"

All the time, as she sang, Madam Mesmer gazed at the audience hungrily, longingly. Almost, realized Jonas, as if she was trying to put them under a spell. The crystal swung backwards and forwards, backwards and forwards before the upturned faces. Jonas felt as if everyone around him was gripped by those mesmerizing eyes. In fact, if he hadn't been looking round to check if Scraps was all right, he might have been transfixed himself.

With a triumphant laugh, Madam Mesmer flung open the doors of the medicine chest, revealing rows of glinting glass bottles.

"Just buy it and try it!" she murmured, holding up this bottle of medicine, that jar of ointment, this box of pills. "My cures will ease every known disease."

Each item was declared more of a miracle than the one before. Madam Mesmer seemed to be able to aid every ailment anyone could name. As if in a dream, the people passed forward their money into Octodious Ollett's outstretched hand. As he bundled the cash into the greasy satchel, they clutched desperately at the small items they got in return.

A burly bargee who had arrived late to the scene surged forward. "Eh up, what's she saying?" he protested. "That's a right load to pay for liniment!"

Jonas felt the spellbound crowd shiver, as if they were coming to their senses. Just in time a wretched figure, face hidden in a rough shawl, crawled from the crowd up on to the stage, and lay there shrieking. It was wrapped in pitiful rags from head to foot.

"Ah! What do I have here? A withered wreck, wracked with pain," Madam Mesmer crowed, pointing a purple-ringed finger at the quivering shape. The audience stared open-mouthed at the pathetic figure.

Ollett selected a bottle from a shelf in the medicine cabinet, and rushed forward.

He tugged out the stopper with a flourish, and held it to the lips of the feeble creature. As the liquid drained from the bottle, the creature fell back as if dead. The crowd gasped.

Then the trembling began. First feet, then legs, arms, body, head – as if life was filling the figure once more. Up sprang the miracle cure, straight and strong, spouting joyful thanks for Madam Mesmer and her Medicines.

Jonas felt cold as he watched this marvellous miracle. He'd glimpsed, below the pitiful rags, two bruised ankles. He knew who it was who'd crept, disguised, on to the stage at that critical moment. When he heard Lizzie's voice sing out "Cured! Cured! Cured at last!" Jonas shook his head sadly.

He hated what Lizzie was doing – fooling the crowds, faking miracles, making Mesmer's medicines seem to work when they probably didn't – but he could not hate Lizzie. Jonas was sure she had no other choice.

"But all the same, why does she do it?" he thought angrily. He could not see how to help her.

The amazed audience burst into a roar of applause, and began loading themselves with more of Madam Mesmer's potions and lotions. Whatever their ailments or illnesses, she was sure to sell something to cure it! Sickened by the sight, Jonas jumped down from the fence-post, waking Scraps from his snooze. The little dog wagged his stubby tail eagerly.

"Come on, Scraps!" said Jonas, almost ashamed of himself for leaving Lizzie. "Time to go home!"

The afternoon sun was sliding lower in the sky already. Jonas checked that the packed sledge was secure. As he urged Ruff, Tuff and Greytail on their way, he could not help puzzling. At least now he knew why Lizzie hated people staring at her.

Hebbing Bridge was left behind, and soon

the heavy sledge was sliding past the Common. He glanced at the small camp in the purpling shadow beneath the trees. The old horse and donkey cropped hungrily, desperately, at the meagre grass poking through the snow. Surely Lizzie was the person who'd ridden on his sledge, not the cunning, tricky creature she became for Madam Mesmer's show? He sighed, setting his mind to the trip home.

The drag back up Highover Hill was harder than ever, and the journey over the snow-covered moor was bleak. Jonas strode beside the hounds when the roads were steep, and he rode the loaded sledge when the lanes were level. All the time, his heart felt almost as heavy as the sledge.

By the time Jonas got back to Rickety Hall, it was late evening. He unloaded the sledge silently. He did not want to talk to anyone about his trip, or about Lizzie Linnet. Not yet.

chapter 5

Jonas put all the parcels outside the right rooms. Then he sat down with a comforting mug of hot chocolate. As he sipped, he could not stop thinking about Lizzie. He'd seen her when she stood on the milestone. He was sure she longed to fly, to escape. So why didn't she?

By dawn the show would be travelling on. Madam Mesmer wouldn't wait for folk to find out that her expensive cures were just coloured water and stinking soaps. So where would Lizzie be in a week's time? In a day's time? It was already too late to help.

Scraps pattered up to Jonas, snuffled in his pocket, and tugged out a soggy sheet of crumpled paper. Jonas took the blue sheet and unfolded it. It was the poster that Octodious Ollett had wanted so badly! It was advertising Madam Mesmer's Marvellous Medicine Show, but not the show they'd seen at Hebbing Bridge! That scam was over and done. The next show, Jonas read with growing interest, was going to be at Riddlesden, the little town on this side of the moors, the town that was close to Rickety Hall itself!

"Good dog!" said Jonas, as Scraps proudly chased his stubby tail round and round.

Of course! Furious folk would come to get their money back if they discovered where the next performance was being held. That was why Ollett wanted the poster to stay a secret, and that was why Madam Mesmer's Medicine Show would keep well out of sight, travelling around the low lanes until they arrived at Riddlesden in – Jonas checked a rather chewed corner of the poster – three days' time!

* * *

All that night Jonas tossed and turned. Even though he knew what it was like to live a rough life, he didn't know how to help Lizzie. When morning came, he went down the long corridor, and knocked on the library door.

"Yes?" said the beardy old man inside. He was sitting at his desk, beaming a welcome. He put down his pen, blew the ink on his notebook dry, and peered over his glasses. "Now, what do you want, young Jonas?"

"Supposing," said Jonas, scratching his head, "supposing you knew someone might be in trouble, what would you do about it?"

"Oh, rickety-rackety, what a thing to ask!" chuckled the beardy old man, pointing to a row of leather-bound encyclopaedias. "I'd find out more about it!"

"You're probably right," admitted Jonas.
"But those books won't be any use for what
I'm after. I'll have to go and look for the
answer myself."

All that day, Jonas got on with things as
fast as he could, because tomorrow – the
second day – he planned to start searching.

So the next afternoon, Jonas and Scraps set
off on the road towards Riddlesden. Madam
Mesmer would be setting up her camp today.
Jonas reckoned he knew where. There was

some wild land just outside the town. People called it Poachers' Patch.

Sure enough, the caravan and small wagon were there, close by a large tree. Jonas and Scraps crouched in the bushes, surveying the scene. A ribbon of smoke rose from the camp, and the foul smell of medicine-making tainted the wintry air. The donkey and horse were snatching wearily at the tough grass. They were so worn out by hauling their heavy loads that they needed no tethering.

After a short while, Jonas spotted Lizzie edging out from under the caravan. She crept towards the donkey and nuzzled its long nose, rubbing its sore shoulders. Then she turned to the horse, and muttered in its ear. In one light movement, she leapt on to its back.

Out from the caravan rushed Ollett, waving Madam Mesmer's long cane in his hand. He grabbed Lizzie's ankle hard and tugged her to the ground.

"You wasn't thinking of going, was you, Lizzie lass?" he sneered. "Cos if you was off with your old horse and donkey, we'd find you easy. Too old to travel quick, aren't they? We'd see their hoof-prints clear as clear."

Lizzie twisted in his grasp as if she longed to run, but Ollett only laughed.

"And if you run off without your two darlings, little Lizzie, they're done for! We'll send your Bray and Dobbin to the knacker's yard, and they'll be in the glue-pots in no time!" He shook her hard. "So you'd better do what me and Madam Mesmer say, hadn't you? Nobody's going to help you now."

Ollett stamped back to his cart, swinging and swishing the cane. Lizzie slumped sadly on the cold ground. Jonas desperately wanted to go across to her, but if Ollett saw him, it would mean more trouble. What could he do?

Jonas thought for a moment. Then he grinned, leant over and whispered to Scraps.

The little dog's tail wagged merrily. Dropping down on his round belly, Scraps scuttled his way through the snow, each wriggle taking him closer and closer to Lizzie.

Jonas saw Lizzie startled as she recognized his little dog. She looked around the Patch very cautiously, as if she was afraid that Ollett was still watching. Scraps tugged gently at her shawl, gave a soft growl, and wriggled his way back towards Jonas. Lizzie's eyes followed the small dog's trail.

After a minute or so, she stood up, idly, and took hold of Bray's trailing rope. She led the donkey towards a crop of frosted thistles close by Jonas. The donkey could hardly hobble. Lizzie did not turn towards the bushes, or show she knew anyone was around.

"So, Jonas," she asked, under her breath, "what do you think of me now you know what I do? Play-acting to part poor people from their pennies?"

"Lizzie, I don't think less of you," he whispered back. "You stay for the sake of Dobbin and Bray, that's what I think."

She shrugged. "Maybe."

"Maybe?" he queried.

"Jonas, what else can I do? Where else can I go?" she retorted. "My Ma and Pa were rope-walkers and one day their rope snapped. That's all there was to it. Nobody wants to know about high fliers that fall to earth." Lizzie gave a deep sigh, then covered it with a bright, brittle smile. "Forget what I said, Jonas. Takes away from folks' fun at the fair."

Jonas watched Lizzie's face. This wasn't any play-acting.

"Of course, Madam and Ollett was nice as plum pies while they spent our savings, and Ma and Pa got worse..." her voice trailed away.

"So you've truly got nowhere to go?" Jonas asked.

"Nowhere that would take my old Dobbin and my poor Bray. Nowhere that would take a tricking, tale-telling moll like me. Ain't that a fact, Jonas?" Lizzie Linnet's face came over hard again. "Best not to bother about me, Jonas. Just clear off to wherever your home is, and forget. I'm more trouble than I'm worth."

She turned back towards the caravan. Bray heehawed sadly, and ambled awkwardly alongside her.

chapter 6

All the way back to Rickety Hall, Jonas kept worrying.

"I have to do something about Lizzie, but what?" he thought.

As he and Scraps went up the stone steps, and entered the huge front door, the grandfather clock in the hall started striking the hour.

"Woof, woof!" Scraps barked, tugging at Jonas's trousers to remind him that it was time for tea.

"All right, Scraps! Let me guess. You're hungry?" Jonas said, heading towards the rattle of cups coming from down the hall.

Just before he went into the room, Jonas stopped to glance in the huge gilt-edged mirror on the wall. He looked fairly tidy, once he'd taken a twig or two out of his hair and brushed down his jacket.

The huge lounge was full of books and papers. There was an enormous fireplace, and a large, polished table. Five chairs were arranged around the room. Each was occupied by a rather odd-looking old gentleman. A dog lay by each chair. Tall or small, plain or spotted, rough-coated or smoothly furred, the dogs lazed happily in the warmth of the room. Occasionally they glanced up at their rather odd owners, and their odd owners smiled down at them.

Closest to the fire was a sturdy wooden armchair. The beardy old man sat there, with a toasting fork in one outstretched hand. A bread knife and some large loaves stood on a small table beside him.

"Good to see you, Jonas Jones!" he beamed, toasting a thick slice of bread over the flames. He had white hair and a bushy white beard, and wore an ink-spattered jacket. As soon as the toast was done, he tossed it up in the air.

The slice was caught by a very old man with a small straggly beard. He was perched on a high three-legged stool. A scrubbed wooden board lay across his bony knees. His faded smock was daubed with paint, but he spread the toast carefully with butter.

"Very good to see you, young Jonas!" he said, popping the toast on a large oval plate waiting on the table.

A carved wooden chair, decorated with painted birds and animals, was the next seat around the room. The extremely old man sitting in that place grinned at Jonas.

"Extremely glad to see you, extremely!" he said, adding another slice to those already on the oval dish.

Suddenly, he whipped out a small curving stick, and sent the dish skimming the length of the polished surface. It came to a halt against a large, erratic metronome, where an exceedingly old man was in charge of the jam jars. Rhythmically, he dropped glistening spoonfuls of jam on each slice. "Exceedingly glad to have you here, Jonas!" he sang.

On and on the old men worked, until a hundred slices seemed to be dancing their way around the room. Gradually, the toast piled high on an enormous silver platter, resting on a stand warmed by candles.

Beside this last enormous platter was an unbelievably old man, older than all the rest. Whenever one of the candles went out, the unbelievably old man leant a frail hand over and lit another flame.

"Unbelievably good to have you here, dear boy!" he whispered, winking. "We're all dying for a cup of tea!"

Jonas lifted the kettle from the fire and filled the enormous teapot. Then he went round as cheerfully as he could, pouring out tea, and trying not think about what he had learnt that afternoon.

Everybody crunched their buttery toast and supped their cups, but at last the old men stopped munching and stared hard at Jonas.

"Rickety-rackety, lad, what on earth is troubling you?" they asked.

Jonas frowned. "It's like this," he began, and told them all about Lizzie Linnet and the evil Madam Mesmer. "So what do you think I should do?" he asked.

52

"Well," said the first old man, scratching his beard with a pen. "If I was writing a story, I'd say it depends what kind of ending you're after."

"Or what kind of picture you want to finish with," said the very old man, doodling on his napkin.

"However," said the extremely old man, taking a compass from his pocket, "you have to think what direction you want to go in."

"Or whether you'll be walking or marching?" said the exceedingly old man, tapping a rhythm on the table-top.

"Or what your dream might be?" murmured the unbelievably old man sleepily as he puffed out the candles because tea was over.

Jonas listened to them all, and thought and thought. At last he went up to the tall tower at the very top of Rickety Hall. It had windows on all sides, and the late afternoon sky seemed to glow all around. The room was empty, apart from a shelf high on the wall. On that shelf stood an upturned hat.

Carefully, Jonas lifted the hat from the shelf and peered into it.

There, under a blanket, lay the very oldest old man of all. All of a sudden, he opened his bright eyes and winked at Jonas.

"What do you want, Jonas Jones?" he asked. "You don't look very happy."

"Well," said Jonas. "I've been told so many things today, my mind's in a muddle."

"Rickety-rackety, Jonas Jones," the old man smiled. "There's only one answer. Just do what you know you must do."

* * *

Jonas lay in his bed, looking at the snow fluttering gently down from the night sky. Scraps was snuggled by his feet. He thought and thought. There was only one answer. If Lizzie wouldn't come without Dobbin and Bray, he'd have to rescue them all. How he'd do it was another problem. It would be all too easy for that horrible Ollett to track a trail of hoof-prints through the snow.

That night, as Jonas stirred restlessly in his sleep, he heard Greytail howling at the shining moon, and smiled. A plan had come into his mind.

chapter 7

The next morning Jonas and Scraps set off on foot, down Rickety Hill and into Riddlesden.

"Listen, Scraps," Jonas said, as he heard the pipe music start in the Market Square. "We keep away from Lizzie, right? That horrible Ollett mustn't know we're here. I just need to check out how things are."

"Woof!" said Scraps.

* * *

Jonas watched Madam Mesmer give her Marvellous Medicine Show, and saw again the spell she cast on the crowd with her peculiar purple stare. He saw Lizzie dancing and play-acting. He watched as people queued for syrups for hiccups, for boil-bursting ointments, and pills for odd ills, knowing the medicines would do no good at all. He watched Octodious Ollett grasp the cash greedily. He wished he could put an end to all the trickery, but helping Lizzie was first on his list. After the show was over, Jonas and Scraps hurried back up to Rickety Hall.

* * *

As the afternoon darkened, Jonas got the sledge ready. He eased Ruff, Tuff and Greytail into the harness, and led the sledge silently down the long lanes. Scraps sat happily in the seat. At last they were close to Poachers' Patch. Jonas put his finger firmly to his lips.

"Stay!" he mouthed, and the hounds sank on their hind legs.

Madam Mesmer and Ollett were there, huddled over their pots and pans again. The harsh medicinal smells told Jonas they were preparing more potions to sell. There was a great clashing and crashing of glassware.

"Hurry up, you lazy lump!" cried Ollett. "The sooner we get our stock cupboard full again, the better."

Jonas, hidden behind a stumpy tree, saw Lizzie struggling wearily with a basket of bottles.

"Start labelling up, miss, and be quick about it!" Madam Mesmer yelled, waving a ladle about, and splashing some stinking brown brew everywhere. "Once those stupid folks start to complain, we'll have to make…"

"…a swift getaway AGAIN!" Ollett joined in, and the wicked pair chortled with laughter at their plan.

Jonas grinned grimly himself. He had a plan, too.

After a while, the small fire died down. Ollett gave a great yawn and shuffled to his covered cart. Madam Mesmer grabbed at Lizzie's ear.

"I want all this stuff stowed away before you dare sleep," she snapped. Then she staggered into the warmth of her comfy caravan.

Jonas saw Lizzie work wearily on, although it was bitterly cold by now. At last she stashed the final bottle into the medicine chest, and crept quietly across the snow to say goodnight to Dobbin and Bray. Now Jonas had his chance.

When Lizzie saw what was waiting over in

the darkness, she couldn't believe her eyes. She almost cried out, but Jonas shoved his hand over her mouth.

"Not a blooming sound about the sledge," he whispered. "If Ruff, Tuff and Greytail can keep quiet, so can you."

Carefully, quietly, Jonas and Lizzie coaxed old Bray up on to the dog-sledge.

"This way there'll be no hoof-prints to follow!" explained Jonas.

The hounds stood patiently, with slightly astonished expressions on their faces. The bow-backed donkey shuffled about uneasily on the back of the sledge. Her tail twitched to and fro, and she put her long ears back, but Lizzie whispered and calmed her as best she could.

Jonas beckoned the huge hounds, they began to pull, and the sledge began to move. Bundles of brushwood tied behind wiped the signs of the sledge rails from the frosted ground, so there were no tracks, no hoof-prints for anyone to follow.

Dobbin looked up, curiously watching the strange parade of boy, dogs and donkey. The sledge slid along the level snow easily, and turned the corner.

One gone! Lizzie breathed, although her heart was pounding with terror. All she had to do was wait, and that was hard enough.

An owl flew past hooting, and Madam Mesmer's snores turned into spluttering and coughing. Lizzie saw the curtains of the caravan twitch. A huge face with sleep-shut eyes appeared for a second, then sank away again. Madam Mesmer had been too asleep to focus but her slumber-thick voice called cruelly out across Poachers' Patch.

"You still fussing around those bags of bones, girl? Is that horrible horse still standing?"

Dobbin whinnied back in answer.

"And the dratted donkey isn't dead yet?"

Lizzie's eyes widened. If Madam Mesmer discovered Bray missing, Jonas's plan would be spoilt. As loudly as she could, Lizzie put back her head. "Heehaw! Heehaw!" she brayed up at the moon, trying to sound as donkey-like as she could, and trying not to giggle.

"Keep those blasted beasts quiet!" Ollett's drunken voice mumbled.

Soon Lizzie heard them snoring again. She eased her aching back against the warmth of Dobbin's coat, waiting for Jonas to return.

The moon was growing pale, and the frost was white as chalk when Jonas reappeared. Quickly, Lizzie led Dobbin over to the sledge, but although the horse had seen the sledge before, it made no difference. He began to roll his eyes in terror, and shake his mane.

"It's no good," said Jonas. "He won't go on."

"I can't ride him," fretted Lizzie. "They'd follow the hoof-prints and find us again."

"You can't ride him on the road," said

Jonas, "but you can ride him up on to the sledge."

So Lizzie swung herself up on to Dobbin's back. Gradually, she coaxed the old horse, one hoof after another, on to the back of the sledge. Dobbin swished his tail anxiously as she tethered him in place.

"Hold it there, Lizzie." Jonas mouthed. He waited for the horse to settle. "Now, pull!" he whispered to the dogs.

The hounds pulled as hard as they could, but the iron runners were wedged in the thick snow. Jonas found a rope from under the seat, tied it to the sledge, and hauled too. The sledge shook a little, but it didn't budge. Lizzie slid from Dobbin's back. The horse stood calmly now, as if he understood what was happening. Lizzie looped another rope around the sledge, and tugged too. The sledge creaked a little, but still wouldn't move. Jonas clenched his fist in desperation. He'd so wanted his plan to work, and he was afraid the creaking would wake the villains. Then Scraps came clambering over the deep ruts of snow, and seized a loose end of rope firmly between his small sharp teeth.

"Again!" whispered Jonas, almost laughing at Scraps's earnest stance.

So they hauled again: Ruff, Tuff and Greytail, Lizzie and Jonas, and little dog Scraps. At last the sledge began to move. Scraps wagged his stubby tail proudly as the sledge slid further and further from Poachers' Patch. The branches behind swished and swept away the trail.

It was only as they dragged the sledge through the great gateposts of Rickety Hall that the wind rose up. It caught Lizzie's bedraggled shawl, tugged it from her frozen shoulders, and tossed it down into a ditch. Lizzie was too cold even to know that the shawl had gone, and Jonas was too busy looking at the way ahead. The shawl settled on the soft snow.

* * *

As dawn broke through the winter clouds, Lizzie, Dobbin and Bray were safely in the grounds of Rickety Hall.

"Welcome," said Jonas, going towards the stone steps. "I'll find a room for you to stay in."

But Lizzie shook her head. "No, Jonas," she said. "I can't stand being cooped up. Don't like houses."

"Well, where then?" Jonas sighed.

"How about over there?" said Lizzie, pointing towards an old rickety barn. One wall was tumbling down, and the tiles had blown off much of the roof. She smiled and wearily waved a hand at Jonas. "We'll be just right in there," she said.

Jonas was too exhausted to argue. He led the sledge round to the stable yard, and tossed bones over to Ruff, Tuff and Greytail as they settled back in their kennels. Then he stumbled back inside the ancient house, and struggled sleepily to his own bed. Everything else could wait until morning. As Jonas dropped into a deep sleep, he kept thinking that there was something he had forgotten.

Scraps sniffed, and nosed around at the crumbs in his empty bowl for a while. Eventually, he pattered up to his special place on Jonas's bed. He curled up tight, and after a while his tummy stopped rumbling.

chapter 8

When Jonas woke, much later that morning, he knew he had a lot to do. He sat up, patted Scraps quickly, and hurried off downstairs. He slipped through the back door and over to the old rickety barn. Lizzie was already awake.

"Will you come into the house for a while?" Jonas asked. "My family will want to meet you."

Lizzie nodded, warily. So they went through the huge front doors, along the hall, past the huge mirror, and into the lounge.

"Rickety-rackety, who have we here?" the

old men asked, looking up from their books and papers.

Jonas told them all about the show and about the great escape. Lizzie gave a shy smile, and shook their hands. They said how brave the pair were, and what a wonderful plan it had been. But when Jonas took Lizzie up to the tall tower, the oldest old man of all only smiled kindly at Lizzie – almost as if, somehow, all the tale had not yet been told.

All this took Jonas a very long time. It felt odd to have someone his own age at Rickety Hall. It was fun to chat and laugh, and show Lizzie all the interesting rooms and objects in his home. With one thing and another, Jonas forgot to put out any breakfast for Scraps.

Ruff, Tuff and Greytail woke and wolfed the rest of their juicy bones. Dobbin and Bray munched on a manger full of oats and hay. Only Scraps scuffled about here and there. By now, he felt very hungry.

Scraps tried sitting by Jonas, but he and Lizzie were busy chatting and laughing. Scraps tried sitting by the old men, in case they had any hidden goodies, but their own dogs growled to warn him off. He tried lazing by the fire, but he just got under everyone's feet. So Scraps went out into the wintry garden. He sulked around the icicle-hung terrace. He scampered over the snow, chasing birds. Soon he was sure it must be mealtime, so he trotted back into the house, his tail wagging.

Still Jonas and Lizzie were chatting. Still his bowl was empty. Scraps's tail drooped. He felt hungrier than ever.

"Woof?" he said. "Woof?"

Absent-mindedly Jonas ruffled Scraps's

fur, and tickled him under his chin. Then he got up, but not to get Scraps his dinner. Jonas wanted to show Lizzie more of the exciting things around Rickety Hall. Scraps padded away sadly, all alone.

He woofled and wuffled around the grounds of Rickety Hall until at last he reached the great iron gates. He sniffed the spot where Jonas had once hidden two lucky sixpences. Life didn't feel so lucky to Scraps today. His ears drooped, his head hung down, and he sniffed sadly.

Which was why he did not see Octodious Ollett sneaking up behind the ivy-covered gatepost.

In the early hours, Ollett had come searching. He'd found Lizzie's embroidered shawl in the snowy ditch nearby, and decided that Rickety Hall seemed a very interesting place to look for lost property. As soon as he saw the little dog, he recognized him as the poster pincher.

Ollett grabbed the surprised Scraps and flung him into a sack. "So we meet again, you miserable mutt," he cackled. The sack thumped and bumped on the hard snow as Ollett ran off to show his find to Madam Mesmer.

* * *

Back at Rickety Hall it was teatime. Jonas peered under the table. He hadn't seen his little dog anywhere. Most unusual!

"I don't know where Scraps can have got to," Jonas muttered.

"When did you last see him?" said the beardy old man.

"Don't know exactly," said Jonas. "He came home with us last night."

"And today?" asked the very old man.

Jonas gave an awkward glance. "He was around earlier, I think."

"Ah!" said the extremely old man. "Who gave him his breakfast?"

"Don't know," said Jonas, looking rather ashamed. "I didn't. Or lunch." He took a deep breath. "I should have," he added in a quiet voice.

"Ah!" said the exceedingly old man, and Jonas sighed.

"Well then?" said the unbelievably old man.

"Let's go outside and look," said Lizzie.

Just then there came a loud hammering at the front door.

"Someone with Scraps?" Jonas cried.

He rushed to the front door hopefully, and opened it. There stood Madam Mesmer and Octodious Ollett.

Smiling horridly, they pushed past him. Madam Mesmer glided along the hall, past the grandfather clock, gazed admiringly into the mirror, and swept into the lounge.

"I have come for Lizzie Linnet," said Madam Mesmer imperiously, swishing her mauve velvet cloak around her feet. "And her animals."

Lizzie gasped, backing away behind the very largest armchair. The old men were watching everything – especially Jonas – intently.

"No," said Jonas. "Lizzie lives at Rickety Hall now."

"Fine," smiled Madam Mesmer. "Then we will leave now."

Her purple eyes gleamed cunningly beneath half-closed eyelids. Jonas and Lizzie exchanged puzzled glances.

"But you should know we found a little stray dog on the road today," Madam Mesmer added slyly.

"Oh, Jonas!" cried Lizzie, wildly.

Jonas's eyes filled with angry tears. "But you don't need Scraps," he blurted out.

"No. But we need Lizzie, and her ragged nags, don't we? Or how do we move on? Your choice, young Jonas!"

Madam Mesmer turned and swept out of the room. Jonas rushed after her furiously, his fists flailing, and his mouth yelling. He caught Madam Mesmer by surprise. She crashed against the wall, and the enormous mirror shook behind her.

The beardy old man stepped forward and pulled Jonas back. "That won't do any good, Jonas."

Just then the grandfather clock struck. Madam Mesmer smiled. "You have two hours to decide. Scraps or Lizzie?"

"See you soon, smarty-pants!" smirked Ollett. "Next time you run away, you'd better hang on to your shawl, Miss Lizzie!"

Jonas and Lizzie stared at each other.

"It's simple," said Lizzie, with a desperate groan. "I'll go."

Jonas shook his head, but he looked very confused all the same. Lizzie or Scraps? How could he choose?

"No," said the beardy old man. "Sit down, Lizzie. Sit down, Jonas."

"We shall all think about it!" said the very old man.

"And come up with an idea!" said the extremely old man.

"There must be a way out," said the exceedingly old man.

"So there must," sighed the unbelievably old man.

At first, everyone sat and thought. Then they stood up. Then they all sat down again. Then they walked round and round. Then they scratched their heads and sighed.

"Oh rickety-rackety, Jonas, we don't know!" they chorused. "That mean old Mesmer's got us stumped!"

Jonas ran out of the lounge and through all the rooms, then up, up the stairs to the top of the tower. The sky was darkening outside and the candles shone against the tall windows. He reached up to the shelf, and took down the hat as gently as he could. The oldest old man of all was already awake, watching and waiting for Jonas.

"Please," Jonas asked. "What do I do now?"

"To stop that wicked woman with her evil eyes?" his wise voice asked.

Jonas nodded.

"And help Lizzie?"

Jonas nodded again.

"And get Scraps back?"

Jonas nodded furiously, and bit his lip hard. There was an awful pause.

"Jonas," said the oldest old man of all quietly, "what do you see about you?"

"Nothing," said Jonas rather impatiently, as he glanced swiftly around the tower room.

"Nothing but walls and windows."

"Look again," said the tiny old man, quite firmly. "Look in the windows. What do you see?"

Jonas looked at the dark glass of the windows, and suddenly he saw something there, something quite clearly. Slowly an idea popped into his head, and hope filled his eyes.

"Oh!" he said. "I see! Of course."

And he raced downstairs, and told everyone about the plan.

"It'll take some work to get everything ready," he said, "but it might work!"

"Rickety-rackety, so it might!" cried the old men, clapping their hands.

Lizzie frowned uncertainly. She didn't want to be back in Madam Mesmer's clutches, even for a short while. But this idea was the only hope.

"Yes," Lizzie agreed, her voice almost a whisper. "I'll do it. I'll go back."

* * *

So, even though it was dark, Lizzie set off down the snowy roads, leading Bray. Jonas walked beside her, holding Dobbin's tether. The poor creatures moved slowly, wearily. As they got closer to Poachers' Patch, Lizzie turned to Jonas. They crossed their fingers and wished for good luck. Madam Mesmer and Ollett were standing smugly by their campfire, their arms folded. There was no sign of Scraps.

"Now for your part of the deal, please," asked Jonas simply. "Can I have Scraps?"

The evil pair laughed. "Oooops! Sorry. He's asleep in his cage just now," Madam Mesmer shrugged. "You'll have your doggie back when we leave, and not before!"

"Don't want any tricks, you see," sneered Ollett.

Jonas hadn't expected anything better from these villains. He would just have to let the plan run its course. Any fuss might endanger Scraps. He turned to go.

"Take care of Scraps, won't you?" he murmured to Lizzie.

"Of course," she answered, trying to reassure him.

But, for Jonas the journey back to Rickety Hall all alone was terrible.

"I'll get Scraps back safely. I will, I will!" he kept telling himself.

chapter 9

It was, of course, too late for Madam Mesmer to set off for another pitch. She had no choice but to stay at Poachers' Patch overnight. So, just as Jonas hoped, the thought of making more money made her fingertips tingle. Madam Mesmer decided she would stage another Medicine Show in Riddlesden the next day.

Ollett wrung his hands and worried. "But, Madam, won't there be complaints? What about the medicines that haven't turned out right?"

Madam Mesmer glared at him nastily, and

rapped her ebony cane against his knees.
"Have you no faith in my powers, you odious
little man?" she snapped.

So, next morning, Madam Mesmer
polished her crystal ball again, Octodious
Ollett burnished the buckles on his boots,
and Lizzie was sent to check that the shelves
of the medicine cabinet were full. She kept
whispering comforting words to little Scraps,
who was trapped tight in a wicker crate.

And, at the same time, Jonas went
hurrying here and there, down in the high
streets and low streets of Riddlesden, saying
what had to be said.

* * *

By midday, Madam Mesmer's Medicine Show was set up in the Market Square once more. A crowd had collected around the gaudy stage. They seemed the same as usual, except for a mischievous expression sparkling in their eyes. Down among them stood Jonas Jones.

Octodious Ollett bounced cockily on to the platform, his smile smug and secure. Lizzie sprang and somersaulted as before, her smile fixed and grim. On the corner of the stage sat little Scraps, dressed in a stupid ruffled collar. His head hung low, and his stubby tail drooped. He did not even look up to see if Jonas was in the crowd.

Ollett trumpeted his fanfare, and Madam Mesmer oozed again on to the stage. She fixed her enormous purple eyes upon the crowd. Her smile was smooth as cream. Again she held her glittering crystal high, and swung it to and fro, to and fro.

She watched for the crowd to sway with its mesmerizing rhythm. Backwards and forwards, backwards and forwards it flashed.

But the crowd did not sway. Instead, someone complained about some medicine. Then another called, and another. Madam Mesmer's eyes glowed angrily, and she stretched to her full height.

"Hush! You will do what I say," she hissed. "You will all do what I say."

The crowd grew unexpectedly quiet, as if they were fixed by her call. As the crystal shone and swayed, she slithered around the stage, and her voice spoke sweet as honey. Her purple eyes fixed even more firmly on her audience.

"You have no power," Madam Mesmer told them. "You have no power!" she chanted, leaning right out over the audience.

"You have no power!" they echoed, although there was a strange note in their words.

An evil leer spread across Ollett's face, and he joined in, too. "You have no power. You have no power…" he chanted.

"Now!" Jonas shouted, as loudly as he could. "Now! Now!" At once, the audience moved apart.

There, facing Madam Mesmer, stood Ruff, Tuff and Greytail, with their teeth bared. Behind them stood the beardy old man beside the old-fashioned sledge. On that sledge stood the gigantic, glittering mirror from Rickety Hall. It blazed like an enormous globe of light, and caught Madam Mesmer in mid-chant.

The mirror sent back her own dazzling reflection. She saw her own evil expression. She heard her own voice chanting, chanting. She was caught by her own crystal, swaying backwards and forwards.

The mirror whirled with lights. Two purple eyes were staring back at her, reflecting her own wicked wishes.

"You have no power!" she told herself.
"You have NO POWER!"

Madam Mesmer gave an awful screech. The crystal tumbled from her grasp, and she covered her vacant face with her hands. Lizzie snatched up the shining orb, and held it tightly. Ollett stood trembling pathetically, unable to believe Madam Mesmer's strength was broken. Now her eyes were pale and anxious, like a small creature caught in the firelight.

"You have no power," she whimpered to herself, as if she did not know who or where she was. "No power. No power."

Octodious Ollett crept towards her, and she grabbed for him. Together they shuffled off the stage. The crowd let out a huge cheer, pleased to have joined Jonas in the cunning trick. Several big lads ran after the wicked pair, pelting them with rotten vegetables.

"We'll get rid of them," a red-faced farmer shouted. "We'll drive them out of town."

"No!" Lizzie wrung her hands, fretting about Dobbin and Bray.

The beardy old man hurried over to the farmer, and urgently spoke in his ear.

"Don't worry yourself," the farmer said, hurrying off with his mates. "That pair won't escape, certainly not with your horse and donkey. You'll have your animals back soon enough, miss."

By now, Jonas had something else on his mind. Desperately pushing his way through the crowd, he searched frantically for Scraps. The little mongrel was still sitting on the stage, whimpering softly. He had chewed the stupid ruffled collar to bits and his head was sunk down on his paws. Jonas hurried towards him.

"Scraps!" he called. "Scraps!"

"Woof?" Scraps barked, as he saw Jonas charge towards him. His stubby tail started wagging, and he tried to jump up.

"Woof, woof, woof!" he barked, as joyfully as any dog could.

* * *

Eventually, by holding out handfuls of oats, the farmers coaxed the hungry animals away from the Patch and back to Lizzie. Much less kindly, Mesmer and Ollett were packed in a tightly locked carriage that rattled and jolted them far, far away.

So all was over in Riddlesden, and it was time to go back along the frosted lanes and up through the white fields, all the way to Rickety Hall. Jonas and Scraps walked side by side. Lizzie strolled between Bray and Dobbin. Ruff, Tuff and Greytail pulled the sledge. The beardy old man walked beside their grizzled heads.

Behind them, perched on the sledge, the

enormous mirror shone like a sun all the way home.

* * *

Later that evening, Jonas carried extra blankets across to the old barn, because more snow was in the air. Scraps scampered close by his heels. Lizzie was sitting inside the barn, watching Bray and Dobbin munching their feed. Their tails swished contentedly as they ate.

Jonas stared. Mesmer's brilliant crystal was twirling in Lizzie's hand.

"What are you doing with that?" Jonas asked, a little alarmed.

"Remembering!" Lizzie sighed.

"Remembering?" Jonas wondered.

"Yes," she said. "You see, Jonas, this crystal used to be my Ma's. When I saw her dancing with it high on the rope, I thought she was carrying a star." She wrapped the crystal in a scarf, and tucked it away safely. "Thank you so much, Jonas Jones."

chapter 10

So the days went by, and Lizzie stayed on in the rickety barn, with Dobbin and Bray. Jonas, with Scraps beside him, got on with this and that, stirring and baking and making. The old men had something important they were working on in the stables.

The snow grew heavier. White flakes began to fall, swirling over the town and the houses, and across the moors. It covered Highover Hill so deeply that the old milestone wasn't seen for months. It fluttered and fell all around the tall tower and chimneys of ancient Rickety Hall.

Then, one special morning, when the bells began to ring, a beautiful tree twinkling with lights was set in the middle of Rickety Hall, and everyone in the house gathered around it.

There were plenty of parcels scattered underneath it, across the carpet, ready for Ruff, Tuff and Greytail to take around the nearby houses. The branches of the tree were hung with presents. Each one had a label. There were gifts for the old men, and for Jonas, and several bone-shaped parcels too. But Lizzie's name was not on any label. She tried not to mind. There was the feast to look forward to, anyway – and it was delicious!

Once they had all eaten, Jonas pulled back the curtains that covered the high window. "Come and look, Lizzie!" he grinned.

Lizzie looked out of the window, and gave a cry of delight. Close by the house, roofed with snow, stood a caravan – the very caravan that had belonged to her Ma and Pa! It was newly painted, clean and bright and cheerful. It stood in a circle of small bright candle-lights. All the old men chuckled and cheered at the surprise they'd made.

"It's beautiful," Lizzie cried with joy.

She ran out across the snow and climbed into the caravan. It was as cosy inside as it looked outside. Lizzie sighed, and sat for a while, nursing her knees. Then, taking the bright crystal from her pocket, she hung it up inside the caravan. The glittering lights danced around the small space like stars.

Inside Rickety Hall, the old men looked happily out of the window at the moonlit snow. Then they turned back and sat down in their chairs.

"A time for gifts, Jonas Jones," they said.

Jonas went over to take the presents down from the branches of the twinkling tree.

Scraps scurried over to help him, and all the sleeping dogs suddenly sat up attentively.

High in the top of the tall tower, a small voice chuckled.

"A time for gifts, indeed, Jonas Jones."